The Teeny-Tiny Woman

A Viking Easy-to-Read Classic

retold by Harriet Ziefert

illustrated by Laura Rader

VIKING

VIKING
Published by the Penguin Group
Penguin Books USA Inc., 375 Hudson Street, New York, New York 10014, U.S.A.
Penguin Books Ltd, 27 Wrights Lane, London W8 5TZ, England
Penguin Books Australia Ltd, Ringwood, Victoria, Australia
Penguin Books Canada Ltd, 10 Alcorn Avenue, Toronto, Ontario, Canada M4V 3B2
Penguin Books (N.Z.) Ltd, 182–190 Wairau Road, Auckland 10, New Zealand

Penguin Books Ltd, Registered Offices: Harmondsworth, Middlesex, England

First published in 1995 by Viking, a division of Penguin Books USA Inc.
Published simultaneously in Puffin Books

1   3   5   7   9   10   8   6   4   2

Text copyright © Harriet Ziefert, 1995
Illustrations copyright © Laura Rader, 1995
All rights reserved

LIBRARY OF CONGRESS CATALOGING-IN-PUBLICATION DATA
Ziefert, Harriet.
The teeny-tiny woman / Harriet Ziefert;
illustrated by Laura Rader.   p.   cm.—(Viking easy-to-read)
Summary: A teeny-tiny woman finds a teeny-tiny bone
in a graveyard and takes it home to make soup,
but changes her mind during the night.
ISBN 0-670-86048-4
[1. Folklore—England. 2. Ghosts—Folklore.]
I. Rader, Laura, ill. II. Title. III. Series.
PZ8.1.Z55Te 1995 398.2'094102—dc20 [E] 94-43813 CIP AC

Viking® and Easy-toRead® are registered trademarks of Penguin Books USA Inc.

Printed in U.S.A.

Reading Level 2.3

The Teeny-Tiny Woman

Once upon a time,
a teeny-tiny woman
lived in a teeny-tiny house.

One nice day,
the teeny-tiny woman
went for a teeny-tiny walk.

The teeny-tiny woman
walked a teeny-tiny way.

She opened a teeny-tiny gate.

She went into
a teeny-tiny graveyard.

In the teeny-tiny graveyard,
the teeny-tiny woman
saw a teeny-tiny bone
on a teeny-tiny grave.

The teeny-tiny woman said,
"This teeny-tiny bone will make
a teeny-tiny soup for my
teeny-tiny supper."

The teeny-tiny woman
put the teeny-tiny bone
into her teeny-tiny pocket.

She went back to
her teeny-tiny house.

When she got home,
the teeny-tiny woman was sleepy.

So she went upstairs
to her teeny-tiny bedroom.

She put the teeny-tiny bone
into a teeny-tiny cabinet.

The teeny-tiny woman
got into her teeny-tiny bed
and went to sleep.

A teeny-tiny voice
woke up the teeny-tiny woman.

"Give me my bone!"
it said.

The teeny-tiny woman was
a teeny-tiny bit scared.

She hid her teeny-tiny head
under the covers
and went to sleep again.

The teeny-tiny voice woke up
the teeny-tiny woman again.

"Give me my bone!"
it said, a teeny-tiny bit louder.

The teeny-tiny woman
was a teeny-tiny bit
more scared.

So she hid her head
a teeny-tiny bit more
under the covers.

Then the teeny-tiny voice said,
a teeny-tiny bit louder still,

"Give me my bone!"

This time the teeny-tiny woman
stuck her head out and said,

"Take it!"